Brown Voyage

SCHOOLCATIONS

written by:
Jayde Brown
Jay'Elle Brown
Jayson R. Brown

illustrations and book layout by:
Tammy B. Brown

B.R.O.W.N. Voyage, LLC
Brownies Reaching Others with Narratives
Atlanta, Georgia, USA

Illustrations and Layout: Tammy Brown

Library of Congress control number: 2021923580
ISBN: 978-1-7356195-1-4

www.BrownVoyage.com
thebrownvoyage@gmail.com
Facebook: @BrownVoyage
Instagram: @thebrownvoyage

SCHOOLCATIONS

Hi there! We are known as the Brownies. We are siblings and we love to go on "schoolcations". That's like a vacation, but we also learn new things about different places around the world!

But here's the best part - we get to learn all about the amazing things that make each place special! We try new foods, learn different languages, and explore unique traditions. It's like having a super fun class, but with a global twist!

We want you to come along with us on our next adventure. Let's explore the world together and discover all the incredible things it has to offer!

And don't forget your passport - it's like a magical book that lets you travel anywhere you want. Plus, you get a special stamp every time you visit a new country! It's like collecting amazing souvenirs from all around the world.

You may need a special visa and COVID vaccination card to enter some countries, so be sure to research first. Are you ready? Let's go!

BRUSSELS AIRLINES

28 JUN 2017

ABCD **ARRIVED**

0123 Belgium

UNITED STATES OF AMERICA

Washington, D.C.

28 JUN 2017

ARRIVED (0123)

UNITED STATES OF AMERICA

* ARRIVAL *

REPUBLICA DEL ECUADOR

24 JUL 2018

S123S

ABCD 1234

ARRIVED 16 OCT 2017

COSTA RICA

1234

Egypt

CAIRO

28 JUN 2017

Departed

IMMIGRATION

ABCD 0123

VIRGIN ISLANDS

28.06.2017

DEPARTED

FRANCE

PARIS

DEPARTED

25 AUG 17

PARIS AIRPORT

IMMIGRATION

ABCD 0123

SENEGAL

28.06.2017

DEPARTED

PASSPORT CONTROL   PASSPORT CONTROL

* ARRIVED *

ABCD Honolulu (0123)

28-06-2017

HAWAII.HAWAII.HAWAII.HAWAII.HAWAII.HAWAII

28-06-2017

GHANA

24-JUL   ARRIVAL   ★   2018

UNITED KINGDOM

LONDON

AIRPORT

PASSPORT CONTROL

DEPARTURE

2017-28-06

ABCD   0123

JOHANNESBURG

INTERNATIONAL AIRPORT

ET345 TOKYO ET345

JAPAN

ARRIVED:12 JUL17

ARRIVAL

INT AIRPORT

JAMAICA

25 MAY 2017

239GD ✡ 239GD

JERUSALEM

← ISRAEL →

ARRIVAL

06 AUG 17

CANADA

ARRIVAL

TORONTO

INTERNATIONAL AIRPORT

24 JUL 2018

ITALY AIRPORT

ARRIVED

16 OCT 2017   ROME   16 OCT 2017

IMMIGRATION

ABCD 0123

PERU

28.06.2017

DEPARTED

Jayde, the researcher

I find out about the weather, currency, language, and culture of the places we travel to.

¡GRACIAS!

Jay'Elle, the planner

I find fun activities to help us learn about different places and cultures and make our schedules. This is called an itinerary.

Jayson, the photographer

I take photos so we can share our schoolcations with people, and you can make photobooks of memories.

Welcome to...

AFRICA

5 FACTS

- Africa is big: It's the second-largest continent with lots of different countries and landscapes.

- Cool animals: Africa has amazing animals like lions, elephants, and giraffes living in its parks.

- Rich culture: Africa has many unique cultures, languages, and famous landmarks.

- Long Nile River: The Nile is Africa's longest river, flowing through 11 countries.

- Huge Sahara Desert: The Sahara is the world's largest hot desert, and some animals, like camels, live there.

EGYPT

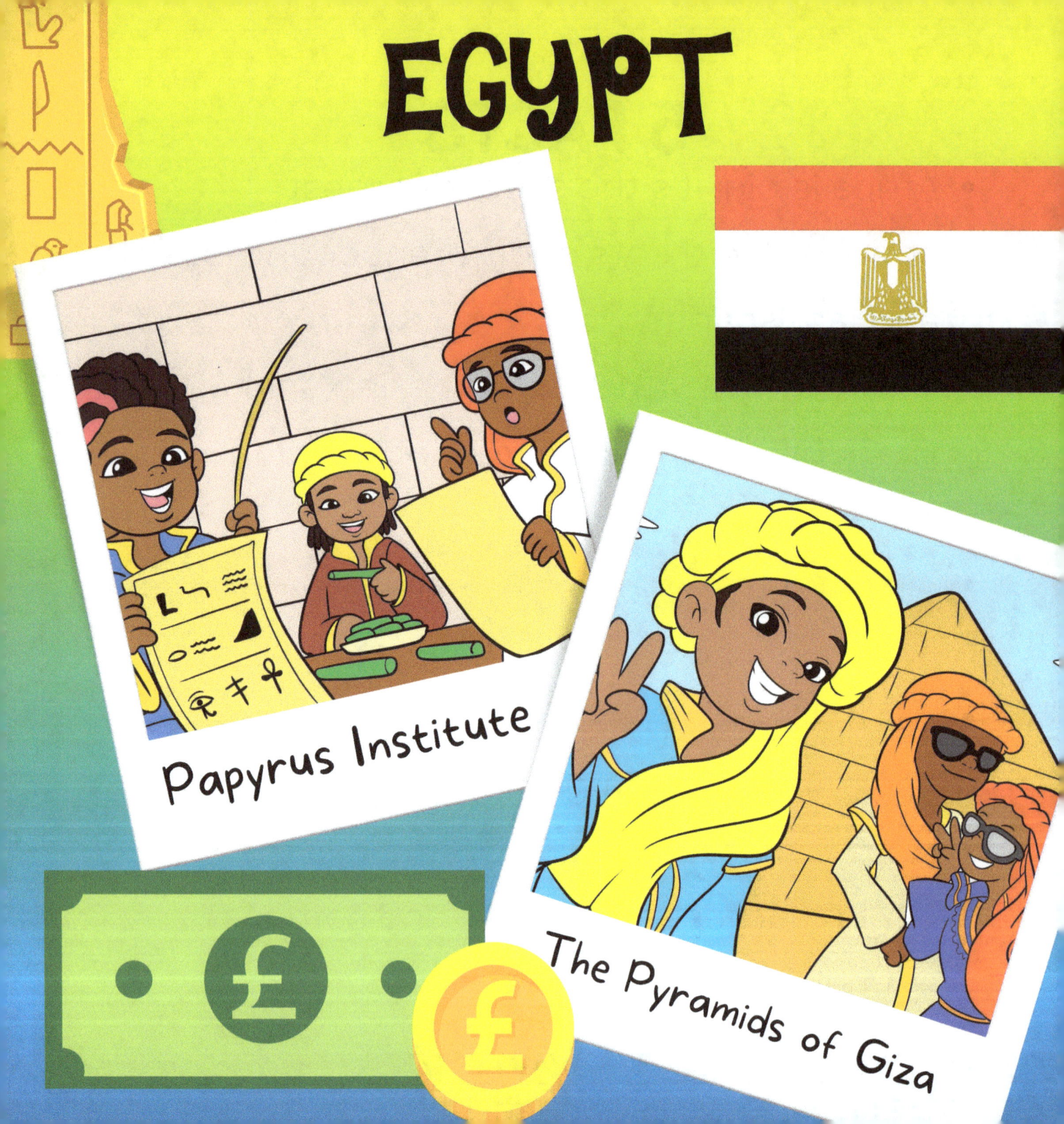

Papyrus Institute

The Pyramids of Giza

As-salamu alaykum! Have you ever heard of Egypt? It's a beautiful country where people speak Arabic. The capital city is called Cairo, and it's the largest city in all of Africa!

The weather is mostly hot and dry, so don't forget to bring sunscreen! And if you want to buy anything, you'll need to use the Egyptian pound.

Egypt is famous for many things, like the pyramids and the Great Sphinx. We even rode camels through the desert to see them up close!

We also visited the Papyrus Institute, where we learned how to make paper out of papyrus, which the ancient Egyptians used for writing! And, we enjoyed eating kofta, a popular sausage dish that was Jayde's favorite meal.

So, if you ever get the chance to visit Egypt, say "Salamu Alaykum" and get ready for an amazing adventure!

GHANA

Independence Arch

Eating fufu and egusi

Akwaaba! Welcome to Accra, the capital of Ghana! This is a special country where people speak many different languages, but English is the main one. The currency used in Ghana is called the cedi, which is important to know when spending money.

During our visit, we tried some of the most delicious local foods like jollof rice, fufu and egusi. It was amazing to try new things and learn about Ghana's traditions.

One of the most important places we visited was called Independence Square. It reminds people about the fight for freedom and independence from the British. It was amazing to see such an important place up close.

We also went on a two-hour car ride to visit Cape Coast Castle. This is a very special place that is important to remember the history of the slave trade. It was a sad reminder of the past, but it also helped us learn about how we can make the world a better place.

At a local school, we met some amazing kids who sang beautiful songs for us. We also read books to them and gave them some school supplies. It was a great chance to make new friends and learn about what life is like in Ghana.

SENEGAL

taking a ferry to Gorée Island

The Door of No Return

Salut! Welcome to Senegal! It's a beautiful country with lots of things to explore. The capital city is Dakar, and French is the primary language spoken there. Jay'Elle knew how to speak French, so she helped us communicate with the friendly locals.

The local currency used in Senegal is the West African CFA franc. It's different from what we use at home, but we got used to it pretty quickly!

Did you know that Senegal is home to the tallest statue in Africa? It's called The African Renaissance Monument and is 50 meters tall! It's a bronze figure that represents victory and freedom.

One of the places we visited was Gorée Island. We took a ferry to get there and learned about the House of Slaves. It was a sad place where people were once kept captive. We learned about the history of the island and how it's important to remember the past.

Of course, we couldn't leave Senegal without going to the beach! Jayson was so excited to ride a jet ski in the ocean. We had so much fun playing in the sand and splashing in the waves. Senegal was such an amazing adventure, and we can't wait to visit again someday!

SOUTH AFRICA

Constitution Hill

Constitutional Court

Howzit! That's one way to say hello in South Africa. People there speak eleven different official languages. When you arrive in South Africa, be sure to get some rand, the local currency. You'll need it to buy all kinds of things while you're here.

We explored the city of Johannesburg on a two-story hop-on hop-off bus, and our favorite stop was Constitution Hill. It's a special place where we learned about South Africa's journey to democracy.

Did you know that Nelson Mandela was once jailed there? He was a brave and important person who helped to end segregation in South Africa.

We also tried a delicious dessert called Malva pudding. It's like a cake-like pudding that can be served with ice cream or whipped cream. Yum!

South Africa is an amazing country with a rich history and culture. It has three capitals: Cape Town, Pretoria, and Bloemfontein. We hope you have a great time exploring and learning more about this special place!

Welcome to...

ASIA

5 FACTS

- Huge continent: Asia is the largest continent, with many countries and diverse landscapes.
- Unique animals: Asia has special animals like pandas, tigers, and elephants living in its forests.
- Amazing culture: Asia is full of different cultures, languages, and beautiful landmarks.
- Tallest mountain: Mount Everest in Asia is the tallest mountain in the world.
- Longest wall: The Great Wall of China in Asia is the longest wall ever built.

ISRAEL
(Middle East)

Cable car to the Mountain of Temptation

Mud bath in the Dead Sea

Shalom! Welcome to Israel! This beautiful country is located in the Middle East, and its capital city is Jerusalem. The official currency used here is the new Israeli Shekel. Israel is a unique and special place known as the Holy Land to both Jews and Christians.

Did you know that the Dead Sea is the lowest place on Earth? It's a one-of-a-kind body of water that's so salty that people can easily float on it, just like a boat! We enjoyed taking a mud bath, which is known for its health benefits.

We also rode a cable car to the top of the Mountain of Temptation and saw breathtaking views of Jericho, the Dead Sea, and Jordan. Jericho is one of the oldest cities in the world, with a history that goes back thousands of years.

We also visited the Church of Nativity in Bethlehem, a town located just outside of Jerusalem. It's believed by many to be the birthplace of Jesus Christ, and it was a truly special and meaningful experience.

Israel is full of wonder and history, and we hope you get the chance to explore and discover all the amazing things it has to offer.

JAPAN

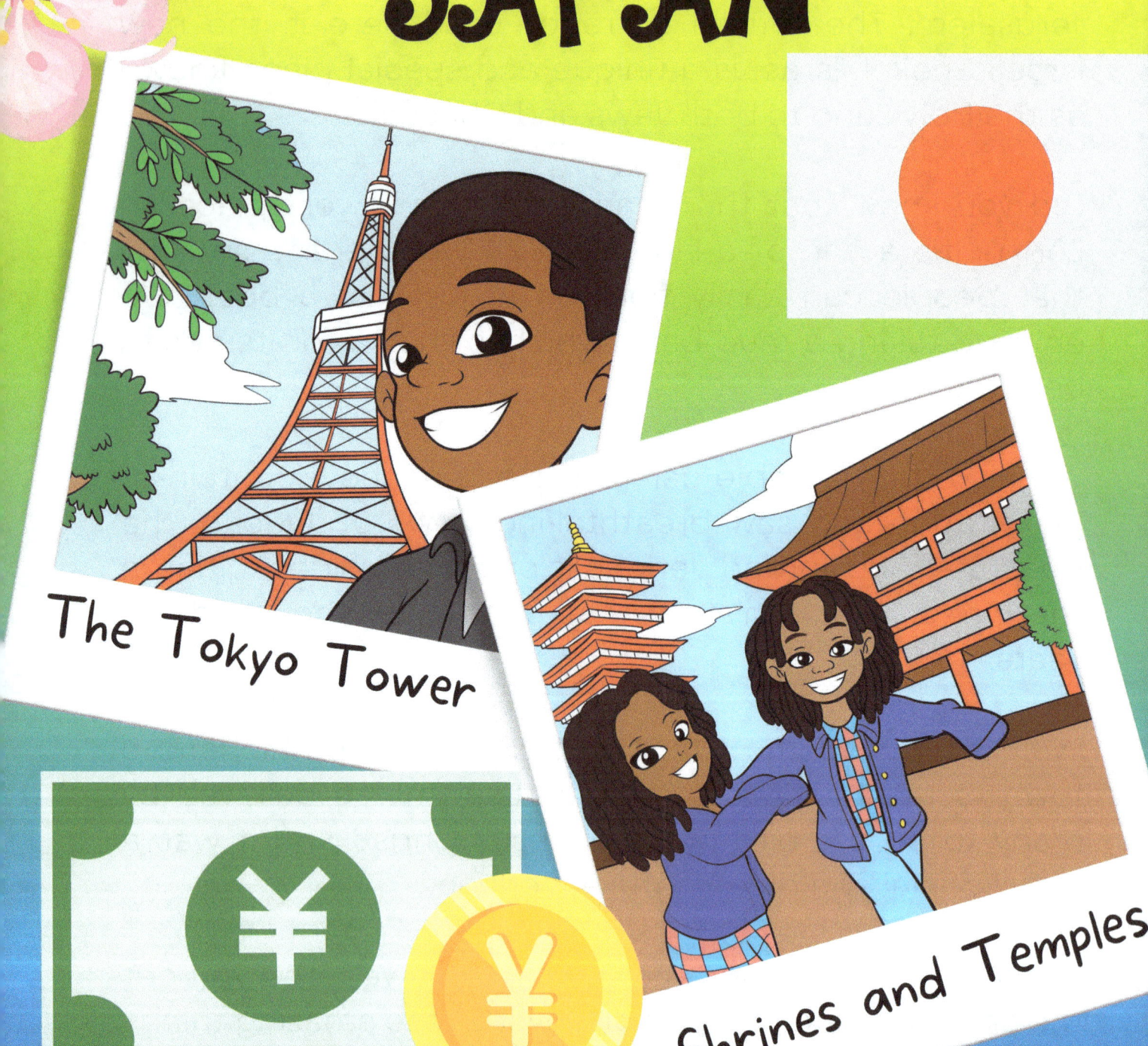

The Tokyo Tower

Shrines and Temples

Kon'nichiwa! Welcome to Japan! The capital city of Japan is Tokyo, and the official language spoken is Japanese. People use the Japanese yen as their currency.

Japan is famous for cherry blossom trees and delicious sushi. We were lucky to visit during the cherry blossom festival in the springtime and see the beautiful blossoms. We also visited stunning shrines and temples during our stay.

The Tokyo Tower is a famous landmark and the second-tallest building in Tokyo. It's an important part of the city's radio and television communication. We took an exciting elevator ride 250 meters to the top of the Tokyo Tower and enjoyed beautiful views of the city.

Our favorite place in Tokyo was Character Street, an underground mall full of shops featuring all kinds of popular characters. Jayson was especially excited to shop at the Pokémon store there!

Japan is a magical and fascinating country, full of amazing food, culture, and traditions. We hope you get to visit Tokyo and experience it all for yourself!

Welcome to...

EUROPE

5 FACTS

- Smaller continent: Europe is the second smallest continent, with over 40 countries close together.

- Cool animals: Europe has animals like deer, foxes, and bears living in its forests.

- Rich history: Europe has lots of famous landmarks, art, and historical events.

- Tallest peak: Mont Blanc in Europe is the highest mountain in the region.

- Many languages: People in Europe speak more than 200 different languages and have unique customs.

BELGIUM

Choco Story
THE CHOCOLATE MUSEUM

The Waffle Factory

Grand Place

Goeiedag from Belgium!

Belgium is an amazing country with so much to see and do. Did you know that the capital city is Brussels, and the currency they use is the euro?

Most Belgians are bilingual, which means they can speak two or more languages. The languages spoken here are Dutch, French, German, and English.

One of our favorite things to do in Belgium was to visit the Christmas Market at the Grand Place. The lights were so beautiful and made the whole city feel so festive!

We also had a fun time learning about chocolate at the Choco-Story Museum. We learned how chocolate is made and got to taste some too. Yum!

And of course, we couldn't leave Belgium without eating some delicious waffles at the Waffle Factory. They were so tasty, especially with a cup of hot cocoa on the side.

Belgium is a wonderful country with so much to explore and experience.

FRANCE

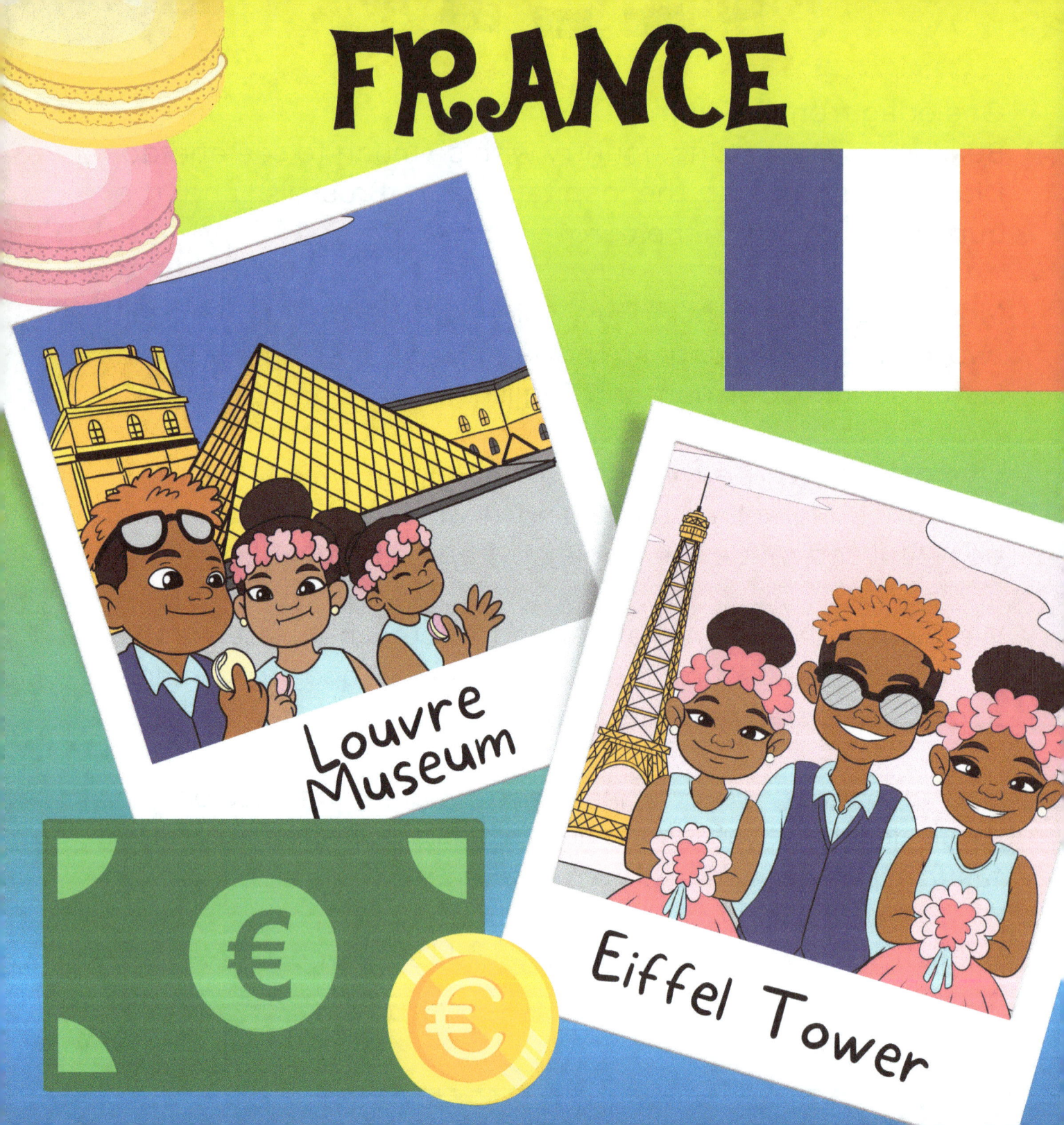

Louvre
Museum

Eiffel Tower

Bonjour! Welcome to France! The official language spoken here is French, and people use the euro as their currency. The capital city of France is Paris.

Paris is known for its famous Eiffel Tower and the world-renowned Louvre Museum. The Eiffel Tower is a romantic symbol for people all over the world, and we were lucky enough to celebrate our parents' wedding anniversary there.

The Louvre Museum is one of the most popular museums in the world and home to the famous Mona Lisa painting.

In the winter, we had a great time ice skating under the Eiffel Tower. We also enjoyed some of our favorite Parisian treats like croissants and macaroons. They were absolutely delicious!

France is a stunning country filled with art, culture, and history. We hope you get to experience the magic of Paris and everything else this amazing country has to offer! Au revoir! (That means "goodbye" in French!)

ITALY

The Colosseum

The Vatican

Ciao, and welcome to Italy! The capital of Italy is Rome, and the official language spoken here is Italian. People in Italy use the euro as their currency.

Italy is famous for its beautiful buildings like the Colosseum and the Vatican, where the pope lives. We were amazed by the stunning paintings at the Sistine Chapel in Vatican City, which is the smallest country in the world!

When in Italy, you can't miss out on trying their delicious pasta, pizzas, and gelatos. We tried different flavors of gelato and enjoyed some pizza at local cafés.

Jay'Elle planned a fun day of exploring Rome on a hop-on-hop-off bus. Our favorite stop was the Colosseum, where gladiator battles took place during the Roman Empire. It was incredible to see this ancient structure up close.

Italy is full of history, culture, and delicious food, and we're sure you'll love it just as much as we did. Buon viaggio! (Have a good trip!)

UNITED KINGDOM

Buckingham Palace

riding the London Tube

Hello there, mate! Welcome to England, also known as the United Kingdom! The capital city is London, and the official language spoken is English. The money used here is called the pound sterling.

One of the coolest ways to get around London is by riding the London Tube, an underground train system. We rode the tube to see some of London's famous landmarks like Big Ben and London Bridge.

We also had a blast riding the classic red double-decker buses. We got off at Trafalgar Square, a big plaza in the city with cool artwork, monuments, and restaurants.

We couldn't leave London without visiting Buckingham Palace, the royal family's home. We learned so much about the history and traditions of the royal family during our visit.

London is an exciting city with lots to see and do. We hope you have an awesome time exploring all the cool things it has to offer! Cheers!

Welcome to...

NORTH AMERICA

5 FACTS

- Big continent: North America is the third-largest continent, with many countries and landscapes.

- Cool animals: North America has animals like bison, bald eagles, and grizzly bears.

- Mixed cultures: North America combines native, European, African, and Asian cultures.

- Grand Canyon: North America's Grand Canyon is a huge, colorful natural wonder.

- Great Lakes: North America has the world's largest group of freshwater lakes.

CANADA

Toronto, Canada

C$ C$

Niagara Falls

Hello and Bonjour! Welcome to Canada, a magical country full of adventure and wonder! Did you know that Canada is the largest country in North America, and its capital is Ottawa? People here speak both French and English, and they use Canadian dollars to buy things.

We had a blast at Niagara Falls, a famous waterfall that can be found in both Canada and the United States. We wore bright red raincoats and went on a boat ride to the falls. We got so close that we got completely soaked! It was super fun.

Have you ever tasted poutine? It's a yummy dish made with French fries, cheese curds, and gravy, and it's very popular here. Jayson loved it so much that he ordered extra fries on the side!

Canada is a beautiful place with friendly people and unique landscapes. Did you know that it has three territories and ten provinces, each with its own special culture? Come and discover all the amazing things that Canada has to offer!

HAWAII

Storyteller Statue

Hawaiian Luau

Aloha, are you ready to explore the magical land of Hawaii? The capital of Hawaii is Honolulu, and the main languages spoken here are Hawaiian and English. The currency used in Hawaii is the U.S. dollar.

Our family visited the Pearl Harbor National Memorial, a very special place where we learned about the events that started World War II.

We also went on many walks and explored and saw the Storyteller statue. This statue is very important to the native Hawaiians because it reminds them of their past and culture.

On Christmas day, we enjoyed a traditional Hawaiian party called a lū'au. It was a feast with delicious food and entertainment. Jay'Elle even learned how to do the luau hula dance, which was so much fun!

Hawaii is a magical place with friendly people and unique traditions. It has lots of beautiful beaches, volcanoes, and colorful flowers everywhere. We hope you get the chance to visit and explore all the amazing things that Hawaii has to offer!

UNITED STATES
Washington, DC

Howard University

US Capitol Building
Rep. John R. Lewis

Hello and welcome to Washington, D.C., the amazing capital of the United States of America! People here speak English, and they use the U.S. dollar as their currency.

Washington D.C. is home to many famous landmarks, such as the White House and the U.S. Capitol. We were lucky to get a special private tour of the US State Capitol from Representative John R. Lewis, who was an important person in the civil rights movement.

We also visited Howard University, which is a special type of college called an HBCU, or Historically Black College and University. It was amazing to learn that Vice President Kamala Harris studied at Howard University. We explored the different buildings and landmarks and learned so much about the rich history and culture of Howard University.

Did you know that the Smithsonian Institution has almost 20 museums and the National Zoo, and all are free to visit? Washington D.C. is a magical city with so much to explore and discover. We hope you get the chance to visit and learn all about the amazing history and culture of the United States!

Welcome to...

THE CARIBBEAN

5 FACTS

- Island paradise: The Caribbean has more than 7,000 beautiful islands surrounded by crystal-clear waters.

- Colorful sea life: The Caribbean has amazing coral reefs with lots of fish and sea creatures.

- Rich history: The Caribbean has a mix of cultures, including native, African, and European influences.

- Pirate tales: The Caribbean was once a popular spot for pirates and their treasure-filled adventures.

- Music and dance: The Caribbean is famous for lively music and dance styles, like reggae and salsa.

JAMAICA

Jamaica

kayaking in Montego Bay

J$

J$

Wah gwaan, and welcome to the beautiful island of Jamaica! Jamaica is a special place where people speak both English and Jamaican Patois, a unique language with its own special words and phrases.

The capital city is called Kingston, and you'll be using Jamaican dollars when you buy things here. Did you know that Jamaica is famous for its delicious jerk chicken and callaloo, a yummy green vegetable that you can taste during your visit?

We had a blast playing in the turquoise waters and kayaking in Montego Bay. Jayson was a natural at kayaking and had so much fun!

One of the most exciting things we did was visiting a local school and making friends with some of the students. We also explored the Rose Hall Great House, which is from the eighteenth century, and learned all about the Europeans who lived there. It was an amazing experience!

Jamaica is a fun and friendly place with many surprises waiting for you. Come and explore all the amazing things this island has to offer!

US Virgin Islands

Mountain Top

Coki Beach

Hey there, from the beautiful island of St. Thomas! This island is a part of the US Virgin Islands, which is a US territory. The capital city is Charlotte Amalie, and the official language spoken here is English. The U.S. dollar is used as the currency.

We drove around the island in a jeep, which is only 13 miles long. Our last stop was the famous Mountain Top, the highest point on St. Thomas. We were amazed by the stunning view of the island from up there!

Coki Beach is a very famous beach here, and there are many sergeant major fish in the water. Jayde had an exciting time feeding them and watching them swim around.

We also visited the University of the Virgin Islands, a Historically Black College and University (HBCU). It was fascinating to learn about the school and its history.

St. Thomas is a magical island with so much to discover. We hope you get the chance to visit and explore all the amazing things that St. Thomas has to offer!

Welcome to...

CENTRAL AMERICA

5 FACTS

- Narrow region: Central America connects North and South America with seven small countries.

- Tropical animals: Central America has animals like monkeys, sloths, and colorful birds.

- Ancient history: Central America is home to Mayan ruins and other fascinating landmarks.

- Rainforests: Central America has beautiful rainforests filled with plants and wildlife.

- Active volcanoes: Central America has many active volcanoes, like the Arenal Volcano in Costa Rica.

COSTA RICA

Costa Rica

coffee plantation

Hola! Welcome to the beautiful country of Costa Rica, where the sun shines all year round! San José is the capital of this country, and the official language spoken here is Spanish. The Costa Rican colón is the currency used for buying things.

There are so many breathtaking mountains and volcanoes in Costa Rica. The warm weather is perfect for swimming, so we put on our bathing suits and jumped right into the pool!

We tried a popular Costa Rican dish called gallo pinto, which is made with rice and beans, and it was so delicious that we ate it with every meal!

Costa Rica is famous for its coffee plantations too. We spent a day on one of these plantations, learning how coffee is grown and harvested from the bean to a delicious cup of coffee. Mom especially loved the experience!

Costa Rica is a beautiful place with lots of things to explore. Come and discover all the amazing things that this country has to offer!

Welcome to...

SOUTH AMERICA

5 FACTS

- Big continent: South America has 12 countries and a mix of landscapes like mountains and rainforests.

- Unique animals: South America has special animals like jaguars, llamas, and toucans.

- Rich history: South America is home to ancient civilizations like the Inca and many beautiful landmarks.

- Longest river: The Amazon River in South America is the largest river by volume in the world.

- Largest rainforest: The Amazon Rainforest in South America is the biggest and most diverse rainforest on Earth.

ECUADOR

the Equator

llama llama

Hola, and welcome to the fascinating country of Ecuador! The capital city is Quito. This country is located on the equator, so it's always sunny and humid. The official language spoken here is Spanish, and the currency used is the US dollar.

Did you know that Ecuador is one of the top banana producers in the world? And llamas play an important role in moving goods from the mountains to the main roads.

We visited the equator, also known as the Middle of the World. We were able to jump from one hemisphere to another in just seconds. It was so cool! And guess what? We even balanced an egg on a nail head at the equator. Jayde did it like a pro!

We explored the city of Quito on a hop-on hop-off bus and stopped at many interesting places. One of them was the top of El Panecillo, a 200-meter-high volcanic hill. From there, we had an amazing view of the entire city!

Ecuador is a beautiful country with friendly people and unique landscapes like the Andes Mountains. We hope you get the chance to visit and explore all the amazing things Ecuador has to offer!

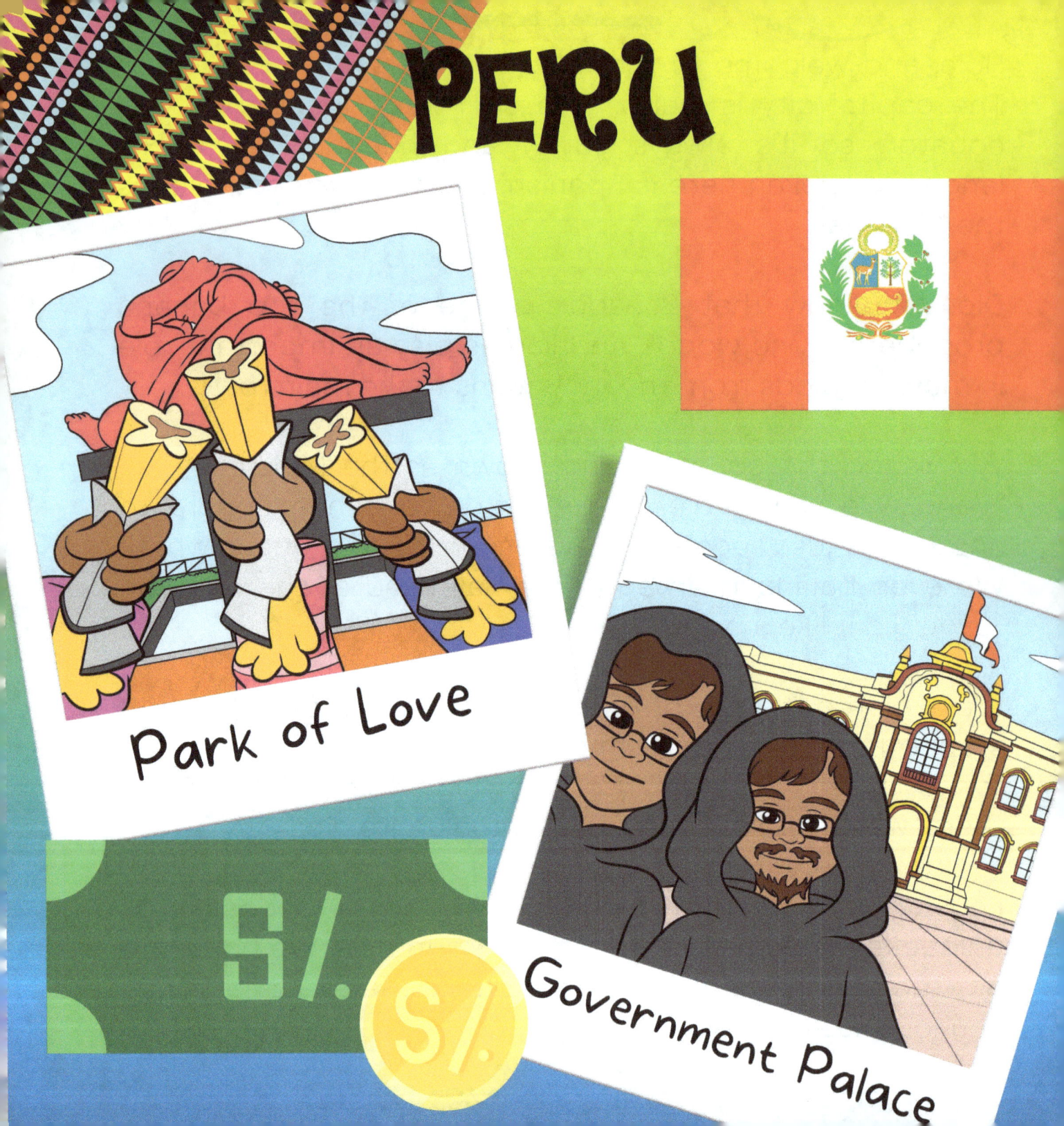

PERU

Park of Love

Government Palace

Bienvenidos to Peru, amigos! Are you ready to go on an exciting adventure to the land of the Incas? Peru is the third-largest country in South America, and its capital is Lima. The official currency used here is called the Peruvian sol, and people speak Spanish and many other indigenous languages.

One of our favorite places we visited was the Government Palace. It was so beautiful, and we even got to meet some friendly monks there. We learned about the history of the palace and saw the amazing architecture up close.

Another fun place we went to was the Park of Love, also known as the Parque del Amor. Jay'Elle planned a special picnic for us there, and we got to eat the most delicious churros while taking in the stunning views.

Our adventure in Peru was filled with so many amazing discoveries and experiences. We hope you'll join us on our next adventure to learn even more about the world!

Use the space below to write about your favorite schoolcation.

Use the space below to draw
your favorite schoolcation.

Jayson Brown

Hi! My name is Jayson Brown, I enjoy acting, traveling, and taking care of my pets. I have three Pomeranians, turtles, tortoises, a bearded dragon, a leopard gecko, and fish!

Jayson Brown

Jay'Elle Brown

Hi! My name is Jay'Elle Brown. I enjoy acting, traveling, and of course, thrifting! I also have an online shop, www.bxtrajayelle.com, where I promote girls' empowerment and mental health awareness.

Jay'Elle Brown

Jayde Brown

Hi! My name is Jayde Brown. I enjoy traveling, acting, and dancing. My favorite dancing styles are ballet and jazz. I also love drawing and enjoy seeing artwork in museums around the world.

Jayde Brown

real photo

University of the Virgin Islands

real photo

Pearl Harbor

real photo

Gorée Island

real photo

the Equator

real photo

Howard University
Washington, DC

real photo

Paris, France

real photo

St. Thomas
US Virgin Islands

real photo

Buckingham Palace
United Kingdom

real photo

Constitution Hill
South Africa

real photo

Costa Rica
South America

real photo

Storyteller Statue
Hawaii

real photo

Washington, DC

real photo

Cape Coast
Ghana

real photo

Pyramids of Giza

real photo

Niagara Falls
Canada

real photo

Dead Sea
Israel

BOOK DEDICATION

This book is dedicated to the memory of John R. Lewis, a true champion of civil rights who inspired so many people to stand up for what is right. The Brown family was fortunate enough to meet him on several occasions, and he was always so kind and welcoming. He even arranged a special private tour of the US State Capitol for us, which was an unforgettable experience. We are deeply grateful for his courage, leadership, and unwavering commitment to justice and equality. John Lewis, your legacy will continue to inspire us and generations to come. Thank you for your tireless work, and may you rest in power.

US Capitol Building

Washington, DC